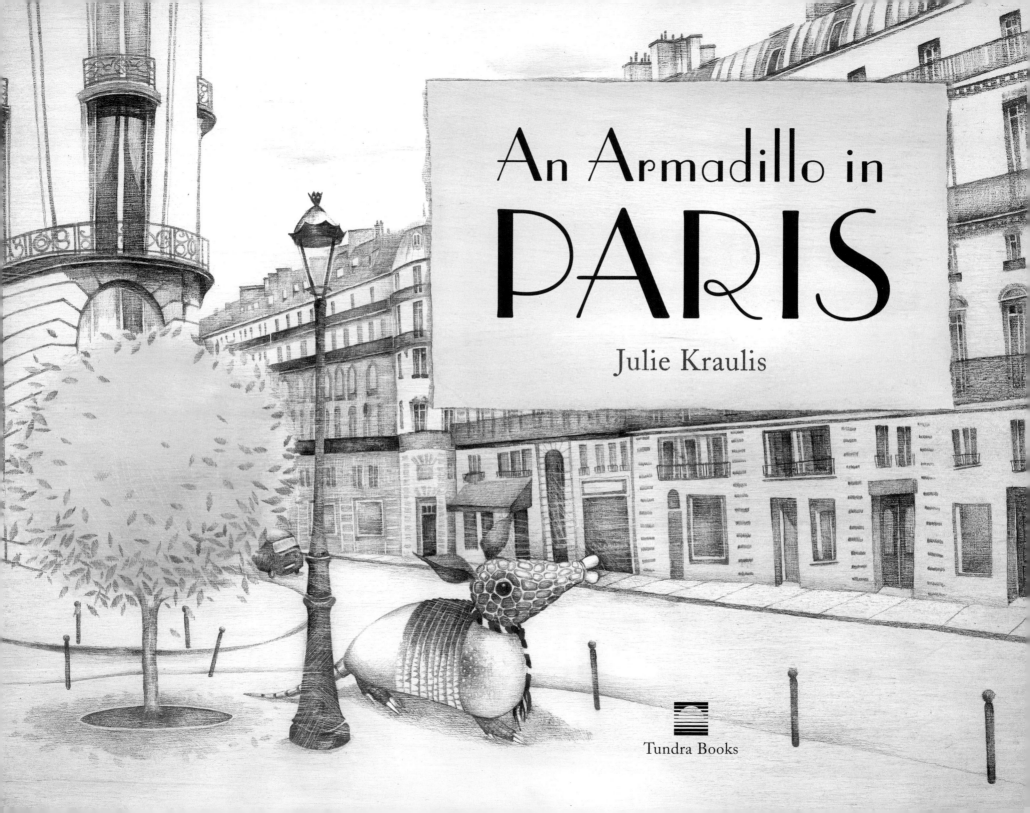

An Armadillo in
PARIS

Julie Kraulis

Tundra Books

For my Grandma Lois and my Grandma Ruth, two great ladies with a spirit of adventure

Text and illustrations copyright © 2014 by Julie Kraulis

Published in Canada by Tundra Books, a division of Random House of Canada Limited,
One Toronto Street, Suite 300, Toronto, Ontario M5C 2V6

Published in the United States by Tundra Books of Northern New York,
P.O. Box 1030, Plattsburgh, New York 12901

Library of Congress Control Number: 2013953674

Library and Archives Canada Cataloguing in Publication

Kraulis, Julie, author, illustrator
An armadillo in Paris / written and illustrated by Julie Kraulis.

Issued in print and electronic formats.
ISBN 978-1-77049-526-5 (bound).—ISBN 978-1-77049-527-2 (epub)

I. Title.

PS8621.R37A76 2014   jC813'.6   C2013-906911-9   C2013-906912-7

Edited by Samantha Swenson
Designed by Jennifer Lum
The artwork in this book was rendered in oils and graphite.
The text was set in Adobe Caslon and Justlefthand.

www.tundrabooks.com

Printed and bound in China

1 2 3 4 5 6 19 18 17 16 15 14

Arlo feels it. The twitch in his left claw. The twitch that only stops when adventure begins. . .

This is Arlo, an armadillo from Brazil. He loves to explore! He inherited his love of adventure from his grandfather Augustin. In fact, curiosity has run in their nine-banded family for as long as anyone can remember.

When Arlo was born, Augustin wrote him a collection of journals about his favorite places in the world so that one day Arlo could use them on his own travels. Today Arlo is reading the journal about Paris and the famous *Dame de Fer*, or Iron Lady, and getting ready to start off on his first adventure!

Dearest Arlo, Paris is one of my favorite cities. I can't wait for you to explore this beautiful place overflowing with art, history and life. You'll love it as much as I do, especially my most favorite thing in Paris: the Iron Lady. Follow the path I've laid out in this journal and you will learn all about her—and even get to meet her! Bon voyage, Arlo.

ONCE YOU LAND, MAKE YOUR WAY TO THE ARC DE TRIOMPHE.
IT IS AT THE CENTER OF A DOZEN LONG STREETS AND IN THE
MIDDLE OF ONE OF THE WORLD'S BUSIEST TRAFFIC CIRCLES. IT IS
THE PERFECT INTRODUCTION TO THE CITY, AND THERE'S QUITE
A VIEW. WATCH YOUR STEP — THE DRIVERS ARE FAST!

After his long flight across the ocean, Arlo catches a ride into
the center of Paris and gets dropped off at the Arc de Triomphe.
He's amazed: it's like being in a whirlpool of cars!

CAFÉ GUSTAVE IS THE PLACE I LIKE TO COME EVERY DAY FOR BREAKFAST WHEN I AM IN PARIS. I ONCE MET A TALENTED ARCHITECT HERE NAMED GUSTAVE WHO DESIGNED THE IRON LADY. HE WAS THE MAN RESPONSIBLE FOR HER WORLDWIDE FAME. THIS IS A PERFECT PLACE TO START YOUR JOURNEY, ARLO. YOU MUST TRY THE PASTRIES!

Arlo starts his day with a flaky *croissant* fresh from the oven. Delicious! He is excited to begin his adventure and his search for the Iron Lady. Who could she be?

YOUR NEXT STOP SHOULD BE THE CHAMPS-ÉLYSÉES. IT IS ONE OF MY FAVORITE STREETS FOR STROLLING AND WINDOW-SHOPPING. PARIS IS KNOWN FOR FASHION, AND THE IRON LADY IS VERY PARTICULAR ABOUT HER WARDROBE. SHE CHANGES HER COLOR EVERY SEVEN YEARS.

Arlo ambles down the street alongside Parisians and fellow tourists. He pauses to admire a beautiful gown in a window. Could this be the color the Iron Lady wears?

You must visit a pâtisserie, a French bakery with all sorts of pastries and sweets. Arlo, I love all sweets, but my favorite is definitely the macaron. They look like buttons spotted, swirled and stacked all over the shop. The Iron Lady loves buttons and has a very big collection!

Arlo gazes in wonder at all of the *macarons* in the shop.
He can hardly believe how many colors and flavors there are.
How will he choose just one? He hopes he will get to see the
Iron Lady's button collection; it must be quite a sight!

Next up is a world-famous museum, the Louvre. Before you go in, stop to look at the Pyramid in the courtyard. It is surrounded by pools of water that reflect it and the ever-changing sky. The Iron Lady is so tall that sometimes she seems to dance in the clouds.

Arlo perches on the edge of a pool and sees his face reflected against the sky. It must be wonderful to be so tall. Maybe when he meets the Iron Lady, he will get to dance in the clouds too.

INSIDE THE LOUVRE, YOU WILL SEE
MANY AMAZING WORKS OF ART.
YOU'LL ALSO FIND THE 1889 WORLD'S
FAIR EXHIBIT. THE IRON LADY WAS
THE FAIR'S OFFICIAL GREETER, AND
IT WAS THE FIRST TIME ALL OF PARIS
AND THE WORLD GOT TO MEET HER.

Arlo explores the rooms filled with historic art — even the world-famous *Mona Lisa*!
The 1889 World's Fair posters and photographs show a very different time. Arlo wishes
he could have been there to celebrate with the Iron Lady.

You should definitely stop at one of the many bridges that span the Seine, the river that runs through Paris. They are a great place for people-watching, one of the Iron Lady's favorite things to do.

Arlo takes a little break on the Pont Neuf to rest his feet. He watches the boats passing underneath and all the people strolling along. So much to see! No wonder the Iron Lady loves it.

Arlo visits the Iron Lady's friends and sees some wonderful things: a church that looks like a wedding cake, some grouchy gargoyles and the colorful glow of stained glass windows. What an interesting collection of friends the Iron Lady has!

HEAD NEXT TO THE RIVE GAUCHE, OR LEFT BANK, OF THE SEINE. IT HAS BEEN HOME TO WRITERS, POETS, PHILOSOPHERS AND READERS FOR DECADES. VISIT A BOOKSTORE AND BROWSE MY FAVORITE SECTION, HISTORY. YOU WON'T BELIEVE ALL THE AMAZING EVENTS THE IRON LADY HAS SEEN!

Arlo meanders through a bookstore. Books are piled to the ceiling and crammed in every corner. What a cozy place!
As he flips through the books, the history of Paris comes alive.
The Iron Lady has seen so many interesting things.

TAKE SOME TIME TO WALK ALONG THE BANKS OF THE SEINE AND LOOK AT ALL THE ART. PARIS IS A CITY FILLED WITH ARTISTS. I LEARNED HOW TO PAINT HERE! THE IRON LADY LOVES ART TOO — HER PORTRAIT HAS BEEN PAINTED MANY TIMES.

After admiring some beautiful pictures, Arlo decides to follow in the Iron Lady's footsteps and have his portrait painted. It will be a good souvenir to take home!

Be sure to visit the Jardin du Luxembourg, or Luxembourg Gardens. It is my favorite park! The light on the pond shimmers like a thousand diamonds. The Iron Lady dazzles like diamonds too, especially at night.

Arlo wanders through the park, joining the fun.
He is mesmerized by the dancing light on the
pond. The Iron Lady must be stunning!

Arlo visits a street market and picks up food for a picnic. He gets enough for two, hoping to share it with the Iron Lady once he finds her.

You're almost there, Arlo. Make your way to the northwest end of Champ de Mars. Stop at Avenue Gustave Eiffel and look up.

The Iron Lady is le Tour Eiffel, or Eiffel Tower! Arlo gazes up at her in amazement. She is the most magnificent tower he has ever seen. He walks over and makes her acquaintance. Just like Augustin, Arlo knows that this is the start of a lifelong friendship with the Iron Lady . . . and with Paris.

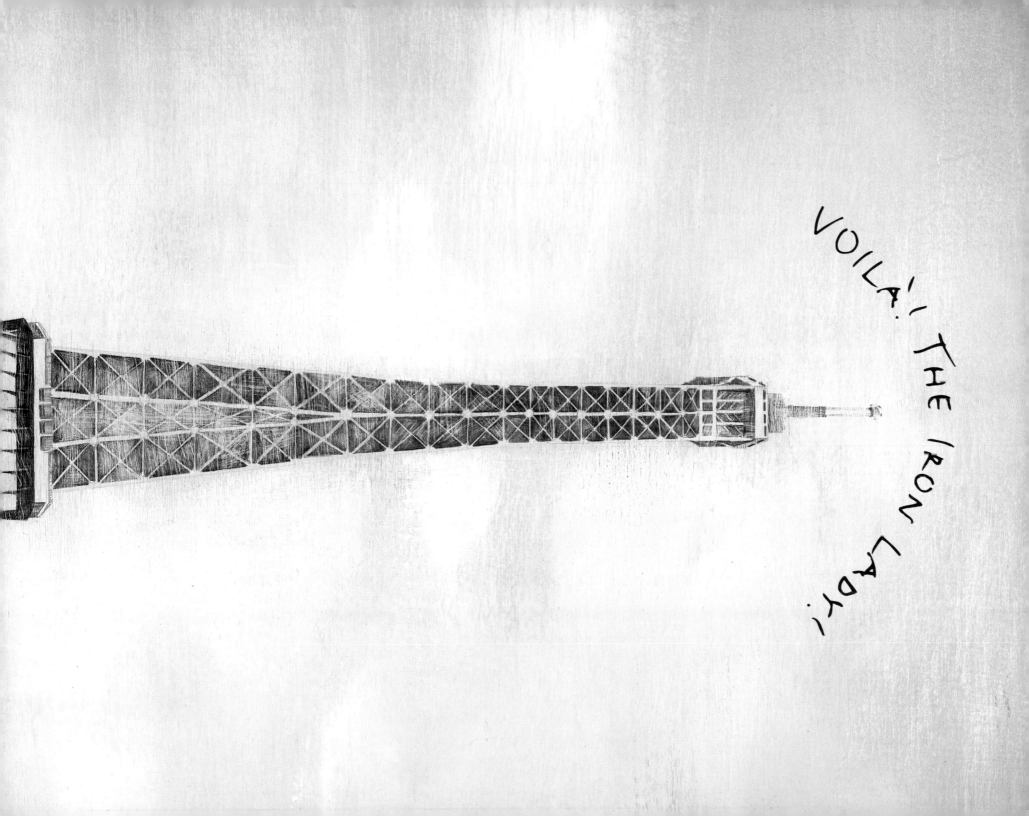

VOILÀ! THE IRON LADY!

ALL ABOUT THE IRON LADY

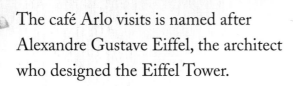

The café Arlo visits is named after Alexandre Gustave Eiffel, the architect who designed the Eiffel Tower.

It's a good thing the Iron Lady likes people-watching. Over 200 million people have visited her since 1889.

The Eiffel Tower is painted every seven years. It takes a LOT of paint! Her three different sections are painted three different shades to accentuate her height: darkest on the bottom and lightest at the top.

Sacré-Cœur, Notre-Dame and Sainte-Chapelle are some of the famous landmarks visible from atop the Eiffel Tower.

The Iron Lady has 2,500,000 rivets or "buttons." That's quite a collection!

The Iron Lady has witnessed many historical events — including the time a con artist "sold" her to unsuspecting buyers . . . twice!

The Eiffel Tower is 324 meters or 1,063 feet tall (including the antenna at the top), which equals 81 stories.

The Eiffel Tower is one of the world's most photographed and painted landmarks. Her likeness has been captured in every season and from every angle!

The Iron Lady debuted at the 1889 World's Fair and was the main attraction. There were long lines to get in; everyone was excited to meet her.

The Iron Lady is covered in 20,000 light bulbs that took 25 mountain climbers 5 months to install. She really does sparkle!